How the Tiny People Grew Tall

How the Tin

People Grew Tall

AN
ORIGINAL
CREATION
TALE

Nancy Wood

ILLUSTRATED BY

Rebecca Walsh

CANDLEWICK PRESS
CAMBRIDGE, MASSACHUSETTS

A *long time ago,* when everything was new, the Tiny People lived in the Center of the Earth. It was hot and crowded.

The Tiniest Person was smaller than the others, only half their size, but he was smart and bold.

"Let's get out of here," he said.

But no one knew how to go about it. They were stuck there in the dark, until one day a star crashed into the earth and made a hole high above their heads. The Tiny People looked up. They saw clear blue sky, and sunlight streaming down.

"If only we could reach that hole, we might get out," said the Tiniest Person. The Tiny People stood on one another's shoulders and made a ladder, but they were still a long way from the top.

One day a corn seed dropped through the hole. As the Tiny People watched, the seed began to grow. At last it poked through the hole.

"Come on," said the Tiniest Person. He swung himself up on a tassel. "Let's go."

The Tiny People pulled themselves up. Their arms ached. They were afraid to be so high in the air. But they kept on going. When the Tiniest Person reached the top, he crawled out and looked around.

"It's beautiful," he said, blinking in the sun.

When the others saw the huge trees and rocks, they covered their eyes.

"We don't like it here!" they yelled.
"We want to go home."
They ran back to the hole.
But it had closed up.
"What shall we do?" they cried.

Animals gathered from far and near to watch as the Tiny People huddled together. "Who are these creatures?" the animals asked one another, never having seen any before.

"Perhaps we should trick them," said Coyote. "I'll ask them into my house, and I won't let them out."

"Perhaps we should help them," said Bear. "They look harmless to me."

"Perhaps we should eat them," said Lion. "They'd make a nice little meal."

"I have a better idea," Eagle said. "Come with me, little ones. I'll take you for a ride to the Sky Kingdom."

The Tiny People didn't want to go, but the Tiniest Person climbed up on Eagle's leg and snuggled down in his feathers. Finally, the others climbed up too.

Eagle flapped his wings and took off. He showed them the world from above.

"See? It's not so bad," he said. The Tiny People enjoyed flying through the sky. They noticed that the clouds were made of dreams.

When Eagle brought them back, he said, "Learn to rise above the earth, like me. You'll see more."

The Tiny People looked at each other, and to their amazement, they had grown a little bit taller. By now they could almost see over the top of the grass. "Thank you," they said as Eagle flew away.

But the strangeness of the world still scared them. So they hid in the hollow of a dead tree.

Then Turtle came crawling by. He noticed the Tiny People stuffed into the tree. "What are you doing in there?" he said.

"Trying to disappear," the Tiniest Person said. The others huddled together. What a big mouth Turtle had!

Turtle crawled closer. There were so many little creatures, each not much bigger than one of his toes. "Get on my back," Turtle said. But most of the Tiny People pushed deeper into the tree.

"Come on," said the Tiniest Person, anxious to see the countryside close-up. He climbed up on Turtle's back. "Let's go for a ride."

"We aren't going anywhere," chorused the others. But they were curious.

Soon one, then the next, climbed on Turtle's back, and off they went.

Slowly, Turtle took them all across the field.
Now and then he stopped so the Tiny People could eat.

They sampled wild berries and found them delicious.

They ate nuts and seeds that had fallen on the ground.

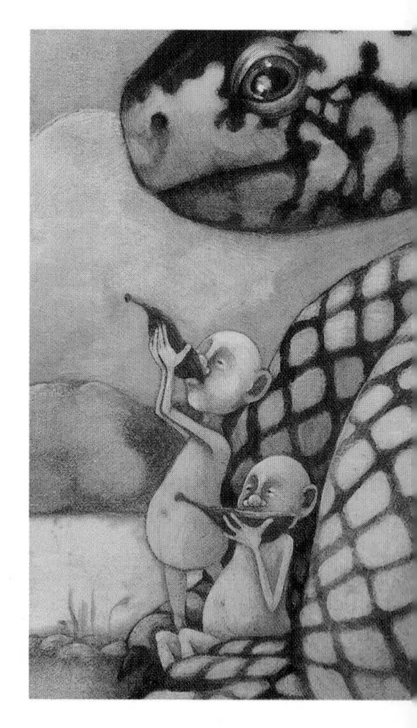

They drank rainwat
from a hollow in
a rock.

When Turtle came to a certain place in the mountains, he stopped. "Here is where you can rest," he said. They slid off and thanked their new friend. Before he left, Turtle said, "You should take your time, like me. You'll learn more." Then he crawled away.

The Tiny People, amazed, saw they once again had grown a little taller. Now they were able to look a gopher in the eye. "You're not so big," they said, but they trembled when he blinked.

A rock still seemed as big as a mountain. The stream was so wide they couldn't see to the other side. Trees were so high they couldn't see the tops. Shivering, they crowded in among a cluster of big red flowers.

Bear stuck his head in the flowers. "Look who's in my Earth Kingdom," he growled.

The Tiny People clung to one another, certain they would be eaten.

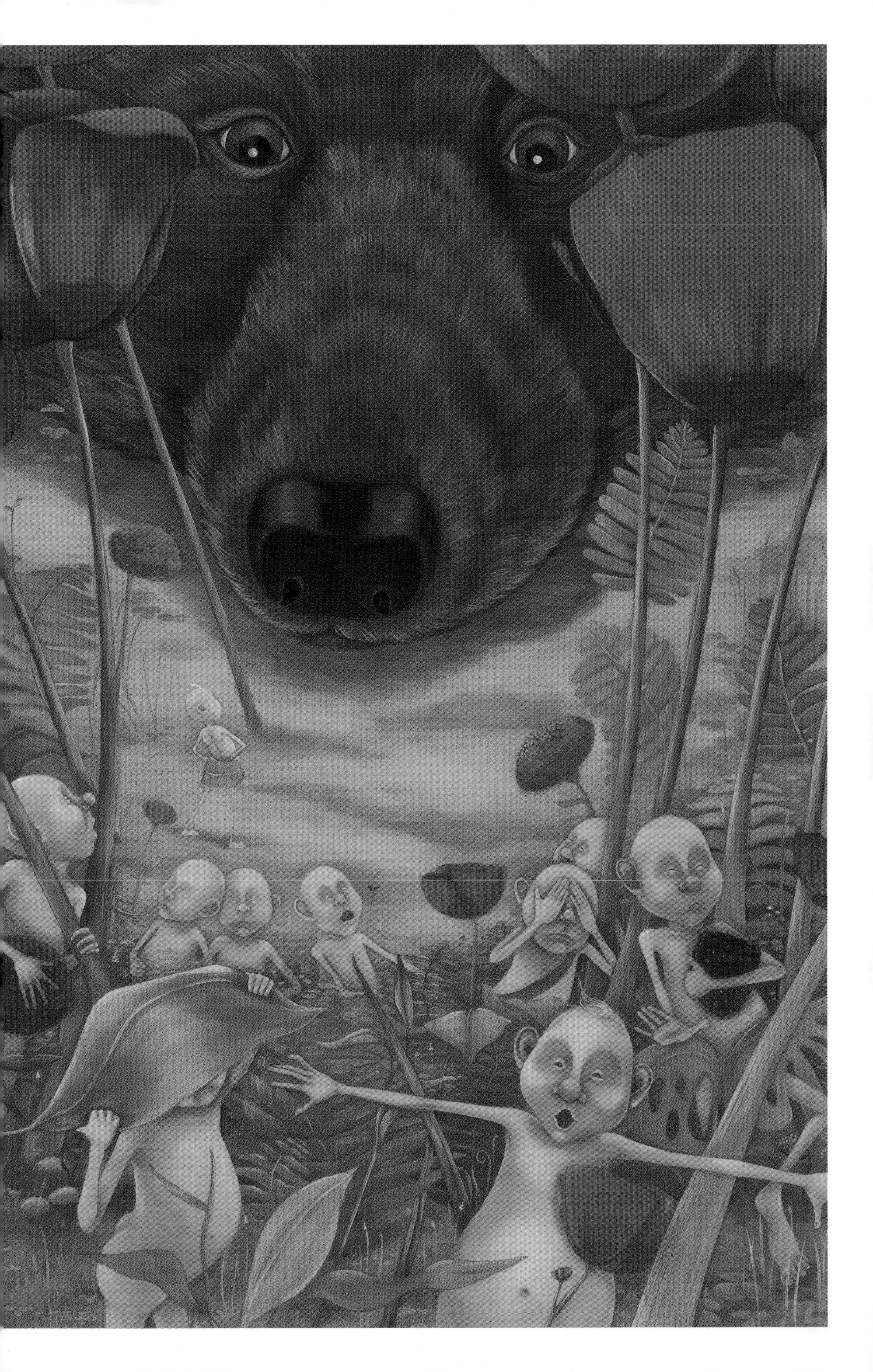

“I am here to help you, not to eat you,” Bear said. “You must be hungry.” He showed them how to gather honey from a beehive. Before he left, he said, ″Learn to be brave, like me. You'll do more.″ The Tiny People thanked him for his help and watched each other grow a little bit bigger still.

By this time, the Tiny People were ready to look for a home of their own. They had traveled far and wide, and had many wonderful adventures. Now they were tired.

Javelina and Roadrunner took them into the desert, but the desert was too hot and dry. Deer and Raven took them to some lush, green land along the river. It was just right.

"Here is where we will live," the Tiniest Person said. He was ready to settle down.

All the other animals and birds now came to help the Tiny People build a home.

Coyote brought them fire in his mouth.

Beaver taught them to build houses out of mud.

Fox showed them how to hunt with tiny bows and arrows.

Magpie showed them how to plant corn. From all these lessons came the knowledge they would need to survive.

After many seasons, the Tiny People grew as tall as young trees. Their skin turned the deep red color of the earth. Their hair was the color of Raven's wings. Their bones were as strong as Bear's.

And the Tiniest Person grew to be the tallest one of all. He was their leader, admired far and wide for his wisdom and courage.

One day, Turtle stuck his head out of his shell and watched the Tiny People having a dance. People learn from animals, he thought. Sometimes animals even learn from people. He knew that it was true.

To my favorite Tiny People, who are growing bigger every year: Ian, Brad, Matthew, Sydney, Ryan, Charles, and Little Timmy

N. W.

To my husband, Nicholas

R. W.

First edition 2005

Library of Congress Cataloging-in-Publication Data

Wood, Nancy C.
How the tiny people grew tall / Nancy Wood ;
illustrated by Rebecca Walsh. —1st ed.
p. cm.
Summary: The Tiny People emerge from their home in the center of the Earth, and what they learn from the animals helps them to grow as tall as trees.
ISBN 0-7636-1543-9
[1. Human-animal relationships—Fiction. 2. Animals—Fiction.]
I. Walsh, Rebecca, ill. II. Title.
PZ8.1.W847Ho 2005
[E]—dc22 2004052143

2 4 6 8 10 9 7 5 3 1

Printed in China

This book was typeset in Meridien.
The illustrations were done in watercolor and acrylic.

Candlewick Press
2067 Massachusetts Avenue
Cambridge, Massachusetts 02140

visit us at www.candlewick.com